Charlie is a dog.

Is Charlie little? No.

Charlie is big,
and he likes to dig.

Look, a log!

He digs under the log.
Look, a frog!

Jump away, little frog!

What did that pup dig up?
It is a red hat.

Funny Charlie!

Who is this?
Who has come?

Help me, Charlie.
Please dig here.

Charlie digs down.
What did he find? It is brown.

Good dog, Charlie!